Kids love
Choose Your Own Adventure !

"I loved the twists and turns of
the different endings."
Karianne Morehouse, age 12

"This is a flashlight-under-your-covers-book
to read at night. It's exciting, thrilling
and fun all at the same time."
Walker Curtis, age 11

"I like the places the author chose to put the
choices. It really makes it hard to put down
the book because it's like you're in the story."
Haley Behn, age 11

"It's really cool how you get to choose the end!
It made the book really fun to read."
Josh Farber, age 12

Watch for these titles coming up in the
Choose Your Own Adventure® series.

Ask your bookseller for books you have missed
or check online at Amazon.com.

RACE FOREVER

BY R. A. MONTGOMERY

ILLUSTRATED BY
SITTISAN SUNDARAVEJ & KRIANGSAK THONGMOON

CHOOSECO

A DIVISION OF CHOOSECO LLC
WAITSFIELD, VERMONT

Race Forever ©1983 R. A. Montgomery,
Warren, Vermont. All Rights Reserved.

Artwork, design, and revised text ©2005 Chooseco LLC,
Waitsfield, Vermont. All Rights Reserved.

Illustrated by: S. Sundaravej, and K. Thongmoon
Book design: Stacey Hood, Big Eyedea Visual Design
Chooseco dragon logos designed by: Suzanne Nugent

For information regarding permission, write to:

CHOOSECO
P.O. Box 46
Waitsfield, Vermont 05673
www.cyoa.com

ISBN 10 1-933390-07-7
ISBN 13 978-1-933390-07-9

Published simultaneously in the United States and Canada

Printed in Canada

0 9 8 7 6 5 4 3 2 1

To
Anson & Ramsey

with special thanks to
Julius Goodman

and to Wick Van Heuven

BEWARE and WARNING!

This book is different from other books.

You and YOU ALONE are in charge of what happens in this story.

Do not read this book straight through from beginning to end! These pages contain many different adventures you can have competing in the First African Dual Road Race Rally. From time to time as you read along, you will be able to make decisions and choices. Your choices will determine whether you win or lose, finish the race or not.

Your adventures will be the result of your choices. After you make your choice, follow the instructions to see what happens next. There are two separate races in this rally, and they are completely different from one another. After you finish one race, you should drive the other to complete the rally.

Be careful! Remember, racing is dangerous. Think before you act. And don't forget that winning is not necessarily finishing the race, nor is finishing necessarily winning.

Good luck!

Epwo m-baa pokin in-gitin'got.

Everything has an end.

-Masai saying

You've been almost too nervous to look out the plane window at the African countryside below. The smiling flight attendant leaning over to check your seat belt jolts you back to reality.

"We're approaching the airport in Nairobi now."

You look out the window. Now you can see the large, modern city below. The gently rolling terrain is unlike the Arizona ranch country where you grew up. You remember the cable that brought you here: "Congratulations. You have been selected to compete in a series of African Road Rallies designed to test both the skill of the drivers and the ruggedness of the cars."

You weren't sure you could handle a race like this, but your dad pooh-poohed that attitude.

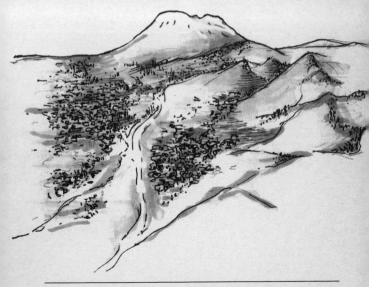

Turn to page 2, and then on to page 4.

4

"Of course you can do it," your dad said. "I taught you everything I know."

And he knows a lot. He and his brother were competition drivers, racing for the Italian Ferrari and Lancia teams during the heyday of the Le Mans, the Mille Miglia, and the Nurburgring races. As soon as you could see over the steering wheel of a Jeep, your father began teaching you about cars and driving. The hours you spent in Jeeps out on the range and in fast cars on the track your dad laid out behind the barn have paid off.

You wish your dad were here with you, but he couldn't come. Some last-minute business forced him to cancel his plane reservation.

At the competition headquarters a large banner proclaiming the First African Dual Road Race Rally flaps slowly in a light breeze. People standing in clumps around a long table are talking excitedly. They are the drivers and navigators, the mechanics, and the representatives of the companies sponsoring this race.

You sign in at the competition desk. "Welcome. Here's your copy of the rules and regulations. I'm Michael Reupleau, race chairman." He smiles at you, shakes your hand, and gives you a large bright blue folder that says Race Kit on the cover. You feel nervous. The other drivers look much older than you and seem very sure of themselves.

Go on to the next page.

"This rally is special," Reupleau continues. "There are actually two races. One tests speed over fast roads in race-prepared cars. In the other race, the rough road race, speed counts, too, but you will be driving off-road vehicles. In each race you will choose your own course, driving from designated checkpoint to checkpoint until you finish. You will not be racing head to head with other cars in either race. Instead, you will select cars and be started at half-hour intervals to avoid head-to-head racing. The courses are too narrow and sometimes too crowded with animals and people for that. Do you understand?"

"Yes, thanks, I understand," you tell him.

"You will be paired with a navigator/co-driver chosen by lot, but that will come in a moment. Now you must choose which race you would like to start with. While you'll take part in both of them, you may decide which race you would like to drive first."

If you drive the speed race as your first race, turn to page 6.

If you drive the rough road race first, turn to page 70.

6

The speed race is a difficult event. It is not like the Indianapolis 500. There isn't a track that you roar around lap after lap. You will start in Nairobi and travel through Kenya. You'll drive along fairly good roads through game preserves, along flat surfaces in the highlands, and through hilly stretches. Finally you'll end up back in Nairobi. You will be out on the roads at least one night during this race, and possibly two nights, depending on what happens.

You eye some of your competitors. The German team is dressed in dark blue coveralls with their names in gold lettering over the breast pocket. They look very serious. The team from Zaire is dressed in tan jumpsuits. Though they are smiling, they look every bit as serious as the Germans.

Now you are confronted with a choice of two cars for this half of the rally. You can choose between a race-prepared Subaru WRX or a race-prepared Audi TT. It's up to you.

If you choose the Subaru WRX, turn to page 18.

If you choose the Audi TT, turn to page 12.

8

Driving at night without full headlights is hard. Your eyes are good, though, and Jan helps concentrate on the dim shapes in front of you, giving warnings when necessary. The driving takes so much attention that it tires you rapidly. You and Jan take turns at the wheel, and that helps a little.

In the darkness, a fork in the road looms. The right fork seems to continue through the valley. It's really hard to see, but the left fork seems to head through the hills up to the highlands. The hills will be hard to drive at night without full lights.

Jan is asleep. A glance at the map confirms what the feeble lights point out. How much time have you made up so far? Which way should you go? The hills are harder to drive, but the map shows that route to be shorter. The valley road is longer, but it will be easier to drive it once the moon comes up.

The decision is yours. Jan must rest in order to be awake enough to take over from you.

If you decide to bear left and head for the hills, turn to page 26.

If you decide to bear right and hightail it through the flatlands, turn to page 29.

Zokil smiles at you, shakes hands, and says, "I am pleased to meet up with you. I saw your name in the race reports. We will do well together. I am sure of that."

You and Zokil examine the Subaru carefully. You give particular attention to the tire treads, which have a special pattern to accommodate the sometimes sandy and muddy roads and the rocky tracks you might have to drive.

"They look good to me. How about to you?"

"I think they're fine, Zokil. They're like the ones we use back home in Arizona."

She suggests you study the map of the course to plan how you will run the race.

"You know, I've been thinking. That Audi could be a little faster. We might have to go all-out to catch up."

You nod. "Perhaps, but if we go all out, we could run into mechanical trouble. There's the wear and tear of high speed on the car, and those roads are really rough in spots."

"Let's decide," she says. "Shall we start out conservatively and count on finishing, or shall we go flat-out?"

If you decide to be more conservative in the race, turn to page 13.

If you decide to go flat out, turn to page 15.

Toward sunset you flick on your lights. Suddenly you hear a crackling sound and smell burned insulation. Quickly you switch off the lights and pull off the road. Investigation under the hood shows extensive damage to the electrical system. "What happened?" you ask Jan, who has almost vanished into the engine compartment, ripping out burned wiring.

"I'm not sure," Jan says. "It looks more like sabotage than anything else. Hand me those pliers, please."

Jan makes the best repairs possible, but the car's lights give only a dim orange glow. They are not at full power.

Now it is getting dark. You need to make up time, but driving at night without adequate light is dangerous. You could stop for a few hours until the moon comes up and use its light, but with the half-hour you lost at the start and the time spent making repairs, that could be the end of your chance to win. If you go on, you won't be able to make great time, but at least you'll get further than you are now.

If you decide to wait until the moon comes up, turn to page 19.

If you decide you can't afford to wait and that your skill will get you through, turn to page 8.

You have chosen the Audi TT. Maybe it will bring you a little luck; you remember your uncle's stories about racing an Audi in the Mille Miglia many years ago.

You check the car out thoroughly. While the mechanics are reinforcing the battery hold-down and doing some other mechanical work you asked for, you discuss strategies with your navigator/co-driver, Jan.

"The Audi's advantage is speed. We should make time while we can," Jan says.

You feel that Jan is right. While you'd rather not push it at first—you want to get acquainted with the car—you decide to go along with Jan's suggestion.

It turns out, however, that you really have no choice. You have to go all out. According to the schedule that you were given when you checked in, you were supposed to start at 3:00 PM. The race officials have erred, though, and officially started their clocks at 2:30 PM.

The starters are adamant and refuse to restart you. "We are officials. We are right," they say.

You have lost thirty minutes because of the foul-up. Once started, though, you fly down the road trying to make up time. The Audi really feels good to you, hugging the curves and stepping right out when you press down on the accelerator.

Turn to page 10.

"OK, Zokil. It is better to finish the race than risk not finishing. We'll race it conservatively."

"Don't worry, my friend, we will do our best to win. You will see."

The race starter drops the flag. The chronometers begin running as you speed off in a flurry of brown-gray dust.

"Watch out for gazelles, Zokil. They're all over the place. I'd hate to hit one; I don't know who'd be worse off."

"Da," Zokil nods.

You settle behind the wheel and resign yourself to the long, grueling hours ahead. Zokil busies herself with the maps, compass, and stop-watches—the equipment of rally navigators. At specially designated points along the route, there will be race officials checking on your progress. You must stop at these checkpoints, for, in addition to checking in with the officials, the stops provide a chance to refuel, make repairs, and rest.

The heat of late afternoon is affecting both of you. It's been six hours of rough driving with no letup. The car is performing well, and it's about time for Zokil to take her turn behind the wheel.

Turn to page 14.

14

Around a rocky outcropping you suddenly come to a very wide riverbed. A trickle of water runs a zigzag course down the middle where the once-large river flowed.

Clouds have been gathering all afternoon. The sky is now a dark gray-blue and thunder rumbles above you. Zokil reports that it's raining slightly to the north. The riverbed is wide and will not be easy to cross. You will have to be careful and take your time. Just then, large raindrops begin to spatter the roof and hood of the car.

You recall a warning of your father's. "Flash flood danger!" you say. "We could get caught out in the middle of that riverbed. Maybe we should wait."

"For what?" Zokil asks. She has never seen flash floods. They can fill a streambed in minutes with a wall of water ten feet high, sweeping away everything in their paths.

If you decide to wait until the storm is over and the danger is past, turn to page 21.

If you decide to risk crossing now, turn to page 24.

"Let's do it. Let's push right to the limit. This car can take it."

You and Zokil get the flag from the race committee starters. You slide through the gears until you are running in fourth along a fairly flat stretch at high speed—the very fastest you can go. The car is well-tuned and responds quickly to your driving skill. The hours melt away and the blazing sun dips in the western sky.

"Fuel is getting low. Maybe it would be good to refuel."

You nod to Zokil and slow the Subaru down, looking for a good spot to pull off the road.

"Over there," Zokil says. "There's a tree to park under. We need the rest, too."

"OK, I see it," you answer.

Soon the car comes to a halt beneath a grove of trees near the road. You get out and stretch your legs to relieve the muscle cramps. Zokil offers you a canteen with a mixture of tea and sucrose.

The extra gas tanks are stored in a rack where the backseat used to be. You hand two of the large red cans to Zokil.

"High speed eats up the fuel really fast. Maybe we'll have to slow down a bit," you say.

Zokil is busy pouring the fuel into the tank through a strainer, an extra precaution to keep dirt from clogging the fuel line or injectors. Meanwhile, you open the hood to check the oil.

Turn to page 16.

Zokil is lifting a jerry can when it slips and hits the ground, spilling gas and spraying it high. Some of the gas hits the exhaust pipe. Immediately it ignites.

BA-RROOM!

Zokil screams. You throw yourself on top of her and knock her to the ground, smothering the furious flames that have started to burn her jumpsuit. Fortunately, the jumpsuit is flame retardant, or it would probably be completely ablaze now.

"Zokil, are you OK? That gas went up so quickly!"

"I'm OK, but my hands and arms are really burned. Look," she gasps.

You examine the reddened, puffy skin where the burning gas has left its mark. You get out the first-aid kit and spread antiseptic cream on the affected area. Zokil says that she is all right now and insists that you continue the race.

You just aren't sure. The burns look pretty bad. The skin is intact; the flames did not penetrate the lower layers of skin, but you think the burns will blister and then could become infected. Also, Zokil is weakened, and she could go into shock. What should you do?

If you decide that Zokil's burns should be treated, turn to page 23, and head for the last village you passed.

If you decide to continue the race, believing that Zokil is all right, turn to page 28.

18

You've chosen the Subaru WRX, a very road-worthy car. As a free agent you've also chosen a stick with the name of your navigator/co-driver on it. You've picked a yellow stick with the name Zokil on it. He must be Russian, you think. You are partly right: Zokil is Russian, but he turns out to be a she!

Turn to page 9.

Perhaps waiting for the moon is best. If you drive at night without enough light, there's no telling what trouble you might run into.

You drive for as long as the twilight holds and then pull off the road to wait for the moon to rise. Jan suggests that you both try to get some sleep. Driving by moonlight will be tiring. You set the alarm on your wrist chronograph and settle down in the grass.

At first the strange night noises keep you from dropping off. You try some yoga relaxation exercises, and before you know it your alarm wakes you.

You and Jan look the Audi over, checking the oil level, tires, and so on. The moon rises above the line of trees in the distance. It is more than half-full, and its pale yellow light is most welcome.

The moonlight allows you to go much faster than you could have gone in the dark. You make good time down the highway.

Go on to page 20.

"There's something in the road ahead," Jan announces, just before you spy it.

"A roadblock," you say. "Must be some government problem."

A tall, uniformed guard motions you to a stop. Before you can ask what this is all about, he tells you to get out of the car.

You look at Jan in surprise. The guard takes this badly and waves his machine gun.

"Out of the car," he says again, menacingly this time. "Both of you."

There's no arguing. You both clamber out. Immediately you are surrounded by gun-toting men.

You take a closer look at their uniforms. "These aren't government men," you whisper to Jan. "They're bandits."

The big guard who stopped you chops his hand down for silence. Then he points his machine gun. The meaning is clear: Go that way.

You head off the road into the bushes and march, in silence, for about ten minutes. Next to a tree the big guard, who is obviously in charge, motions a halt. With a few waves of his machine gun, he directs a young bandit to tie you and Jan back to back with the tree between you. Then the bandits all tromp off about fifty feet through the bushes.

The sound of Swahili drifts over to you. Now you regret that you never learned that language. You whisper to Jan, "Can you understand any of that?" but Jan's eyes tell you no. You wonder what's in store for you both.

Turn to page 33.

You tell Zokil that a flash flood could ruin the race for you. It would be crazy to risk crossing the river now.

"OK, I will listen to you. You are right. It is best to wait." Zokil opens the car door, steps out onto the dry, sandy road, and stretches.

As quickly as the storm clouds gathered, they break and become harmless. The threat of a flash flood is over. Although this is lucky for you, it is actually too bad it didn't rain. It is the dry season, and the moisture would have been useful to the people and animals who live in this part of Africa.

Just as you and Zokil are getting back into the car, the single side-band radio—standard equipment in this race—crackles several times and begins to broadcast.

"Turn it up, Zokil. I can't hear it."

The voice over the speaker is loud, commanding, and very British: "Warning. Repeat, warning to race participants near sector A32. Repeat, sector A32. Reliable sources report that a sizeable band of well-armed guerrilla troops is operating in that area. The race committee recommends a non-penalizing, twelve-hour delay. Repeat, we strongly urge a twelve-hour, non-penalizing delay for all drivers near sector A32. Please radio in your choice."

Turn to page 22.

Zokil stares at you, her eyes clear and her face calm and determined. "Guerrillas! Hah! What would they want with us?"

You hear her question, but you don't answer immediately. You need time to think. What happens if you wait it out in this remote area? You are on the edge of sector A32. The guerrillas could be right around here—or further on. Any way you look at it, there's danger. But when you began the race, you knew there could be trouble along the way.

"Zokil, look. If we stop, we can stand watch and take off quickly if the guerrillas approach. If we leave, the guerrillas will see the dust we kick up for miles."

"Then what should we do?" Zokil asks.

If you decide to stop here and take the non-penalizing, twelve-hour delay, turn to page 35.

If you decide to risk a guerilla encounter and go right on through sector A32, turn to page 57.

"I'm sorry, Zokil. The race is over for us. You've got to get some medical help. We're heading back."

Zokil leans back in her seat. Shadows of pain darken her face. You drive as fast and as carefully as possible, trying not to jar her. The drive seems twice as long as you remember. Finally you arrive at the small village.

The village is spread out around one main hut where the headman—or chief—lives. The other huts, with their yellowing thatched roofs, are placed in a precise arrangement around the main hut. They are only slightly smaller—just enough to symbolize their difference from the headman's hut.

A Jeep with the light blue seal of the United Nations is parked beside one of the huts. To your great delight, you realize that a U.N. agricultural and medical support team is here.

"Hey, we need help! Hello! Anyone here? We need help!"

From the headman's hut step three people dressed in blue dungarees and khaki work shirts. One of them has a short white beard. He is deeply tanned.

"I am Doctor Rudoff. What is the problem?"

"It's my friend, Zokil. She's burned."

Turn to page 41.

"I don't believe it will flood. Let's go," Zokil says firmly. You agree with her reluctantly. Now you begin to drive onto the uneven gravel at the edge of the broad riverbed. After a few minutes, the Subaru bogs down in sand.

"Don't gun the motor. Easy, easy."

"It's no use, Zokil—it won't come unstuck!"

Just then you hear a muffled roaring noise.

Immediately you know what it is. A flash flood is racing down on you at tremendous speed! Suddenly it's right on top of you, black-brown murky water foaming all over and spinning the car around. The sky is dark again. Thunder rumbles in the hills.

What should you do? Swim for the shore or stay with the car?

If you decide to leave the car and swim for it, turn to page 37.

If you decide to ride the flood out in the car, turn to page 40.

26

You take the left fork.

The hills make for hard driving. You are wearing out rapidly. The moon has come up, but it keeps disappearing behind the hills and doesn't seem to help much. Perhaps you should have stayed in the valley where the moon would have provided steady illumination. No matter. Here you are, and you can't go back.

You and Jan have taken turns driving, and you're behind the wheel now. A glance at your chronograph shows that the sun should start to come up in a few hours. Both you and Jan are dead tired. Maybe now is the time to stop and sleep a bit. You've been pushing along at a good speed for hours, and you hope you've made good time.

Go on to the next page.

It's almost time to change drivers, so you decide to wake Jan up and see about stopping.

Jan struggles out of a deep sleep, looks around, and settles back in the seat as you explain the possibilities.

"So," you say, "maybe we should stop for two hours, catch a few winks, and go on refreshed when it's light. What do you think?"

There is no response. Jan is sound asleep again.

If Jan can't stay awake, the burden of driving will fall on you. Maybe you should stop. On the other hand, talking seems to have helped; now you feel pretty alert.

If you decide to drive on, turn to page 43.

If you decide sleep is the safest bet, turn to page 44.

More than anything else you want to finish the race. Zokil's insistence that she is all right and you should go on is enough to convince you. You roar into the cobweb of roads and terrain that make up this part of the speed race.

"Zokil? Hey, Zokil! I don't know where we are. Do you?"

She looks up wearily from the maps. "I'm sorry. I have not been paying attention at all. I don't know where we are either."

You drive for hours. You think you're moving in a straight line, but you keep ending up at the same large water hole. Vultures circle in the sky above you, hoping for the death that signals a feast.

For you two, the race is definitely over. You are really lost. It will take all of your time and effort now just to get out of the maze you are in. Good luck!

The End

Turn to page 70 to start the rough road race.

You swing the wheel to the right and keep driving through the valley. The moon comes up, lighting up the road. As everything gets brighter, you increase your speed.

Switching seats with Jan after an hour, you gaze at the moonlight on the grass and the umbrella trees out the side windows before you close your tired eyes.

Jan wakes you up from a dream about sleeping in a soft bed. Jan apologizes for waking you and says you've only been asleep for about twenty minutes. "We're lost, I think. Look at those mountains. They shouldn't be there."

Jan's right. Those mountains shouldn't be there, if you are where you think you are. Maybe you missed a turn because you were too tired or you couldn't see well enough in the dark. Maybe you should have turned left after all.

What should you do now? Go back to look for the missed turn, or keep going the way you're headed?

If you decide you must be going in the right direction, turn to page 45.

If you decide you are truly lost and need to turn around, turn to page 59.

The car is it, then.

You haven't made it too far when you hear a thud behind you. Quickly you turn and see Jan stretched out on the ground.

"I tripped. I think I've twisted my ankle."

"Can you walk?" you ask, helping Jan up.

"Not too well. You'd better go on without me; I'll slow you down."

Just then you hear a shout from the bandits' camp!

"Run!" Jan says, and run you do—run for your life!

Turn to page 32.

32

The Audi has been pushed off by the side of the road where you were stopped. There are no guards nearby. It is only a few seconds work to remove the grass that camouflages the car from passersby. You quickly slip inside, insert your spare key in the ignition, and, with a short prayer, turn it.

Yes! The car starts right away! The only problem now is which way to go to get help: in the direction you've been going or back the way you came. "Help?" you think. "Why not use the radio?"

You turn the radio on. Nothing! Perhaps the bandits pulled some wires loose, or maybe it was damaged when the electrical system shorted out.

The bandits are close behind now. You must drive one way or the other.

If you decide help is closer in the direction you've been heading, turn to page 48.

If you decide you'll find help faster if you turn back, turn to page 49.

The smell of a cooking fire drifts over from the bandits' camp.

Jan whispers, "My ropes aren't very tight. That guy who tied us up looked awfully nervous."

"Mine are pretty tight. He did yours after mine. He must have been in a hurry to finish.

"I think we have some time," you tell Jan. "See if you can get free."

Several minutes and a few grunts later, you hear Jan say, "I'm free."

Jan has you untied a minute later. Now what should you do? You can hear the bandits laughing. They must be eating.

There is no mistaking the fact that you are in danger. You know you must try to escape—the question is where and how. Should you go back to the Audi and drive away as fast as you can? You're not sure if the car is where you left it or if it's being guarded. You could go on foot. That would be quieter, but the bandits probably know the terrain better than you.

You have no time to waste. The sooner you get away, the more time you'll have before the bandits find out you're gone.

*If you decide to make a break for the car,
turn to page 30.*

*If you decide to steal quietly away on foot,
turn to page 36.*

"I really believe stopping is the smart thing to do," you tell Zokil. "This is a good spot."

Zokil nods in agreement and begins to unpack the food and sleeping bags. The small alpine stove hisses into action, and in a short time you and Zokil are sitting under an umbrella tree with mugs of hot tea. You keep an ear open for the shortwave to monitor the guerrilla activity.

During the night, you and Zokil trade off on two-hour shifts. You are now on your second shift. The night is clear, the clouds are gone, and the constellations are very bright. The hands of your chronograph glow the time: 1:48. Suddenly the shortwave crackles on.

"Guerrilla troops reported active and hostile. Repeat, definitely hostile. Committee now recommends abandoning race. Suggest all racers return to start. Repeat, committee recommends abandoning race. Good luck."

What will you do now? You don't want to drive at night. The headlights are a dead giveaway. Zokil examines the map with a small flashlight.

"You know, my friend, we are more than halfway to the finish. It might be just as safe to continue on and finish as to try to go back. I think we should continue."

Zokil has a good point. Besides, you just might win.

If you follow the committee's recommendation, turn to page 64.

If you are determined to finish the race, turn to page 60.

"Those bandits are no fools," you say. "When they find us missing, they'll probably head for the car, thinking that's where we've gone. Let's go on foot."

You haven't gotten far when you hear shouts from the bandits. They've discovered that you're missing! Soon you hear them on your trail.

"Let's split up," Jan suggests. "That way we have twice as much chance of finding help." You nod, and you and Jan head off in different directions.

Stealthily you thread your way through the bushes. The sound of the bandits diminishes; then you hear shouting. They must have captured Jan.

If you decide to sneak back to see what you can do for Jan, turn to page 52.

If you decide to keep going for help, turn to page 54.

"Let's go. Time's a-wastin'." You and Zokil jump from the car and plunge into the river.

How could this be? One moment earlier it was a dry riverbed; now, a treacherous torrent is rolling along at high speed, carrying with it tree stumps, animals unfortunate enough to have been caught while drinking from the stream, and you!

You swim with the torrent, but at an angle to the bank. The current catches at you and hauls you about like a toy boat. It is due to luck more than to your swimming ability that you're not battered against the rocks and stumps.

Finally your feet bump against the gravel bank. Then you are laying in the brown, foamy, shallow water that is now receding as quickly as it rose. Zokil is about 100 yards downstream. She makes it to shore safely and weakly waves to you. She is as exhausted as you are.

When you look out at the stream, there is no trace of the Subaru. It's gone!

Go on to page 38.

Several minutes later you join Zokil. The sun is out again. It feels good on your cold, wet skin.

"OK, so here we are. No car, no food, no radio, and miles from anywhere."

Zokil smiles and says, "Yes, but we're alive, my friend. We will make it!"

For two grueling days you and Zokil walk back the way you came. Hunger gnaws at you, but there is water to drink in the puddles made by the violent storm. It's dangerous, though. There could be parasites in the water. Your thirst is stronger than your fear, so you drink. Zokil suggests trying to catch some small animal—a small gazelle, perhaps.

"Fine. Then what do we do? We don't have any matches. I'm not about to eat any gazelle without cooking it."

"You will if you have to."

It's probably fortunate that Zokil doesn't catch anything. Two days later you walk into the last checkpoint. You're exhausted, starved, and disappointed, but you're alive. A race committee team is there in a Land Rover with food, water, sleeping bags, and friendship. You didn't win, this time, but you made it back alive.

The End

Turn to page 70 to start the rough road race.

40

You stay with the car as the floodwaters rise. Too bad. That was a very foolish mistake. The full force of the flash flood traps you and Zokil in the Subaru. The car spins over and over in the foaming water.

The End

While Doctor Rudoff dresses Zokil's burns, you introduce yourself to the other two U.N. officials. One is a woman from Israel who specializes in new methods of crop fertilization. The other is a Swede. He seems very interested in your car.

"My name is Sven. You are a driver in the African Road Rally?"

"Well, I guess so," you say. "Looks like we're out of this one. I'm not sure I can really go on without Zokil."

Sven thinks for a moment and then says, "Back in Goteborg, I was a semi-professional race driver. Weekend races, that type of thing. I could go with you. Why not? I will take your navigator's place."

If you decide to take Sven up on his offer, turn to page 66.

If you decide that you can't give up the race, but you want to try going solo, turn to page 68.

You're exhausted, but pushing on is probably the right thing to do. This is a race, after all, and in order to win you must make the best time. You'll will yourself awake, no matter how sleepy you are.

Remembering your past experiences, you decide to drive faster. Maybe the increased danger from driving at high speed will make you feel more alert.

You watch the speedometer climb upward: 120, 130, 140 kilometers per hour. You feel hyper-alert as the countryside flashes by in a blur.

Without warning, your lights go completely out as you round a sweeping right-hand curve. Your experience as a driver enables you to keep the Audi on the road in the almost total darkness, but no experience in the world will help get that elephant out of the way.

Your car explodes within seconds after you crash into the elephant, and the noise and fire stampede the whole herd nearby. The stampeding elephants cause a panic among the wildlife. They join the great rush to escape the flames. At least some of the animals in the area will survive the grassland fire your burning wreck has started.

The End

You decide that stopping is the best idea. Your alertness is already fading. Fatigue hits you in waves of nausea.

At a level spot you pull off the road. You succeed in waking Jan up, and the two of you collapse onto the soft grass. You're both asleep instantly.

Sunlight in your eyes wakes you up suddenly. You must have overslept! Groggily you look around. "Where's the car?" you shout to Jan, and the two of you frantically search the tall grass. The car is gone!

You can see the tire tracks you made in the grass when you pulled off the road, the place you parked the car, and the tracks the Audi made back to the road, but no sign of any other vehicle.

You're sure you would have awakened if anyone had started the Audi and driven it off. Could somebody have pushed the car onto the road and then started it, far enough away that you wouldn't hear it?

But your speculations are meaningless now. The car is gone, and the race is over for you. Maybe you'll have better luck next time, you hope, as you start your long walk to the nearest checkpoint.

The End

Turn to page 70 to start the rough road race.

"We've gone this far," you tell Jan, "so let's keep going the way we're headed."

Five minutes later you regret your words. The mountains loom even closer and look even stranger. You must be lost!

"Wait a minute!" Jan shouts. "Those aren't mountains. They're clouds! The moonlight just makes them look like mountains."

The sun, rising over the plains, shows that Jan is right. You aren't lost after all. You press down the accelerator as the sun lights up the landscape.

Turn to page 46.

46

At about mid-morning the flags of your next checkpoint appear. You stop to check in and gas up before you restart. You've made good time and are doing better than you thought. There's not even any need to fix the lights; if everything goes well, you'll finish before nightfall.

By pushing on through the night you've more than made up the time you lost at the start. The Audi performs perfectly on the last leg. Your driving is superb, and you pull in at the finish to the cheering of the crowd. Congratulations!

The End

Turn to page 70 to start the rough road race.

48

You drive onward. You think a checkpoint is closer that way. Maybe you can continue the race after they send help for Jan.

When you're a few minutes down the road, an explosion in the engine compartment startles you. Fire under the hood! You stop the car and race out with the extinguisher.

As you start to lift the hood, there is a smaller explosion and flames engulf you. You're on fire! Quickly you throw yourself down and roll on the ground. You put the fire out on your body, but it's too late for your face and hands. They are badly burned.

"Now what should I do?" you wonder.

If you decide to stay with the car and hope a rescue helicopter spots the fire before the bandits do, turn to page 58.

If you decide to get going on foot because the bandits must have heard the explosion and started after you, turn to page 61.

You decide to head back. You'll be on a familiar road, so you might make better time.

Suddenly an explosion almost rips the Audi's hood off. Smoke curls out from the engine compartment. You stop the car and, with the fire extinguisher in your hand, carefully raise the hood. Flames leap out, burning your face and hands.

The bandits must have heard the explosion. You've only driven a little way down the road, so they're probably close behind. You'd better leave quickly!

Half-blinded by the explosion, your hands and face in agony, you head away from the road.

In a thicket of trees you collapse, unable to go any further. While you are catching your breath and wishing you had brought along the first-aid kit to treat your burns, the hair on your neck rises. Somebody's watching you! The bandits must have been closer than you thought.

You raise your head and look around. A tall warrior in tribal dress is staring down at you. Slowly you stand up. The tribesman comes closer and closer, and you are certain he will plunge his spear right through you. You stand your ground, though, and try not to show any fear.

He stops just a few feet from you and looks closely at your face. You look back at him as best you can through your swollen eyes. Suddenly, for no reason you can explain, you smile at him.

Turn to page 51.

The tribesman smiles back. Saying a few words in a language you don't know, he pulls a dry gourd out of a leather pouch and hands it to you. You don't understand. He points at the gourd and then at your face, repeating, "Dawa, dawa."

"Burn ointment," you finally realize.

You spread the ointment on your face and hands. A soothing calm results.

Whup, whup, whup! A helicopter appears out of nowhere. Race officials have come to find you. When you turn around to thank your new friend, the tribesman has vanished.

You rush out of the thicket to flag down the helicopter. When you climb aboard, you are reunited with Jan, who was rescued shortly after you left. The officials take you both to the nearest hospital, where a team of Kenyan doctors check you both out.

"Unbelievable!" is the only reaction the doctors have to your speedy recovery from the burns.

When you are discharged from the hospital, you head back to the highlands. You hope to find the mysterious warrior who helped you and learn what that remarkable ointment was.

The End

Carefully you grope your way back to the bandits' camp. You're listening so intently for footsteps that your ears feel as if they're about to fall off. You're listening so hard, in fact, that you fail to spot the bandit pointing his gun at you until you nearly trip over him.

Recaptured! Sheepishly you raise your hands.

At the bandits' camp you are reunited with Jan. Neither of you is very happy with the circumstances of the reunion. You are tied to the tree again, only this time there are three of you: you, Jan, and the young bandit who tied you up the first time. You are tied more tightly than before; the ropes cut deeply into your wrists.

As you wonder what will happen next, the bandit who stopped you on the road says something in Swahili and raises his machine gun.

He pulls the trigger and short bursts hit both you and Jan in the feet. In pain you watch the bandit raise his gun again, and, after a few more words of Swahili, he kills the boy tied up with you. Then he and the other men turn and walk over to their fire nearby.

Through a haze of pain you hear the sound of a helicopter above the trees. It is the race officials! You hope they will spot you, but the camp is well hidden, and they fly on.

Then you lose consciousness and slump against the tree. Infection quickly takes hold of the untreated gunshot wounds, and you never waken again.

The End

In a few minutes you pull alongside them. They greet you warmly and explain that they had decided to wait because of the guerrillas. The taller of the two, Frederick, points to the low-lying distant hills.

"They are out there. I am sure of it. Maybe we should join forces and travel together. There is strength in numbers, *ja?*"

The other German, Arno, nods his agreement. Zokil talks with him about the route and what lies ahead. They spread the maps out on the hood of the dark green Peugeot and begin to measure distance and probable speeds to calculate some estimated arrival times. Zokil strongly disagrees with Arno about which route to choose. He favors staying on the plains, while she wants to head for the outlying hills.

You listen to both sides, look at the maps, and talk once more with Frederick. He repeats that there would be safety in numbers and urges you to join forces. Still, it might be safer to split up and try to sneak through the hostile territory.

If you and Zokil decide to continue on alone, turn to page 62.

If you decide to join forces with the German team, turn to page 65.

"I'd do better to try to get help," you think, as you quietly make your escape from the bandits.

After a few minutes you hear a helicopter approaching. You run out into the nearest clearing and flag it down. It is filled with race officials and Kenyan police who have been alerted to the presence of bandits in the area.

Following your directions, they rescue Jan and capture most of the bandits.

You and Jan decide to abandon the speed race. You've lost too much time, and, after your adventure, you feel you need to recuperate before attempting the rough road race.

The End

When you are fully recovered, turn to page 70 to start the rough road race.

"We've got to keep going, Zokil," you say. "No sense in being sitting ducks for the guerrillas."

Zokil agrees, and so you cross the river and roar up the road over the sandy hill on the other side. The road is narrow and twists for many miles, but then it broadens and runs straight through grasslands dotted with umbrella trees. You are on the Serengeti Plain.

"What's that up ahead?"

Zokil gets out the binoculars and scans the horizon.

"The German team, I think. Yes, I see them now. It's definitely the Germans in a Peugeot. They've stopped."

Turn to page 53.

You stay with the car. Maybe the bandits won't have spotted the fire. Half-blinded by the pain of your burns, you grope for the first-aid kit.

As the burn ointment begins to ease the pain, you hear a helicopter overhead.

When the helicopter lands to pick you up, Jan is inside, shouting, "Are you all right?" The officials must have stopped at the bandits' camp first, picked up Jan, and then spotted the burning Audi.

At the hospital they tell you your face will be all right. The burns will heal, but you might have a scar or two to forever remind you of the Race Forever.

The End

After turning the car around, you and Jan hurry back the way you came as fast as you can. You mustn't dawdle now. If you are really lost, you need to get back on the track as soon as possible.

You can't find any missed turns, but the farther you go, the more lost you feel.

When the sun comes up, both you and Jan climb out of the car to stretch and look around.

You are lost! Well, not exactly lost, because you can see where you are. You're so far off the right road, though, that you'll never make up the lost time.

Sadly, you radio in that you're abandoning the race, and the two of you drive back to the start.

The next day a helicopter ride over your course shows you your mistake. You were on the right course when you turned away from the hills—but when you turned around, you missed the road you had come out on and went the wrong way.

Better luck next time.

The End

Turn to page 70 to start the rough road race.

60

"Let's hit the road, Zokil. We're going on. The guerrillas can't possibly catch us." Zokil grins and throws your bags into the Subaru. The click of the seat belts is reassuring. The motor roars to life, and you're off.

Go for it!

Finish the race!

Just keep an eye out for the roadblocks. It's a little crazy, but you know you are right.

You are!

You and Zokil cross the finish line eight hours later.

You WIN!

The End

Turn to page 70 to start the rough road race.

You start running to abandon the smoking car. In a panic, you think you hear the bandits right behind you, and you run harder.

Suddenly you stumble face forward into some whistling-thorn acacia bushes. You are cut badly. Hundreds of stinging ants cover you almost immediately, and you rush blindly away in panic and pain. You stumble several more times until you finally collapse, unconscious.

The helicopter finds you near sunrise and takes you to a hospital. You lie in a coma for weeks.

When you regain consciousness, you learn that Jan was rescued shortly after you left by an official helicopter. Later, two of the doctors treating you explain that an infection caused by the acacia thorns has set in. You will need plastic surgery, and, even after several painful and expensive operations, your face will never be the same again.

The End

"I'm sorry, Frederick," you say. "Zokil and I think it's best to go on alone. Good luck, and we'll see you in Nairobi."

The Germans shake hands with you and murmur good luck. Then you are off.

Things go well for the first six hours. You and Zokil begin to relax. Then it happens!

Hand-held rocket launchers attack the car from behind the brush. You never know what hit you.

The End

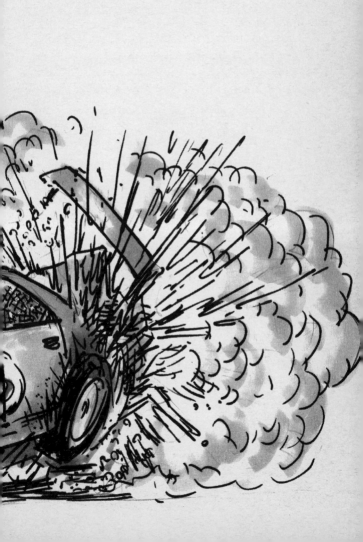

64

You decide to pack it in. There is no dishonor in abandoning the race. It's wise to be cautious, under the circumstances.

"Should we radio in to tell the committee now?" Zokil asks.

"Yes, let's do it, Zokil. Tell them we're headed back, and give them our approximate position and estimated time of arrival. Maybe they'll come out in a helicopter and track us in."

She flips the switch to broadcast and hits the mike button.

"This is Subaru WRX team near the Nagulis River just outside of sector A32. We are abandoning race. Repeat, abandoning race and heading back. ETA to last checkpoint is six hours. Over and out."

Unfortunately for you, the guerrillas have been monitoring the race frequency. They ambush you before you get a mile up the road. You spend the next thirteen months as a political prisoner.

The End

"OK, Frederick," you say, after a few words with Zokil. "We've decided to travel with you. You're right, it's bound to be safer. After all, it's only a race, right?"

"Ja. That is how we feel. There will be other chances to match our skills against one another. Don't worry about that. Remember, we still have the rough road race ahead!"

He smiles and slaps you lightly on the back.

The gear is packed. Oil, gas, water, batteries, and food are checked. Finally you agree upon the route: You will stay on the flat part of the plain.

Frederick says it would be best not to radio in. "You never know where those guerrillas are. They might monitor us."

You nod in agreement. Then the two cars rev up, producing far more sound than you'd remembered. You push in the clutch, drop the gearshift into first, and off you drive.

It's fun driving in tandem—you don't mind it a bit. That is a bit unusual for a race driver.

Fourteen weary hours later your silver Subaru and the green Peugeot cross the finish line at the same time. The race officials congratulate both teams. You did not win, but you finished the race safely.

The End

Turn to page 70 to start the rough road race.

66

"OK, Sven, let's do it. You handle the navigating and I'll manage the driving."

"Good, my new friend. That is an efficient way to handle this race."

Sven smiles broadly at you and indicates with a red felt-tipped marker the route he has chosen. He has been in East Africa doing agricultural forecasting and planning for more than two years, so he really knows the area. The route he proposes is completely different from the one you chose, but you trust his judgment.

Twice you think you must be lost. Small roads seem to turn into dusty ruts that your car can hardly pass through. Then you plunge out of a group of rolling hills onto the plains where a fast road cuts through the flats.

You push the accelerator to the floor, watching carefully. There are cattle along the road, even some zebras.

You dash on as fast as possible, and at exactly 3:21 East African Standard Time you take the checkered flag in Nairobi. You have finished the race third overall!

Zokil meets you at the finish line. Her arms are bandaged and in slings, but otherwise she is fine.

The End

Turn to page 70 to start the rough road race.

You have decided to go on by yourself. It would probably slow you down to take Sven along. You check the Subaru over quickly, looking at the tires and the gas and oil levels. Carefully you trace your route on your maps. The heat of the day lies in shimmering waves on the plain stretching all around you. In the near distance are pale blue hills fringed at the bottom with pale green.

You drive for hours, fighting the sun and your intense fatigue. You become so tired that you forget to eat; the lunches and snacks you and Zokil packed in Nairobi lie unopened.

Shift. Accelerate. Brake. Downshift. Accelerate . . . You must constantly stay alert for the donkey, the lion, the people, and even a frightened gazelle crossing the road.

Will the race ever end?

Shift. Accelerate. Check the gauges. Gas. Oil. Odometer. Clock. Brake. Downshift. Drift. Accelerate. Upshift . . .

Then you see it! The high-rise buildings of Nairobi float like ships above the horizon—white, unreal signals of the finish.

Congratulations! Although you did not win, you finished, something many other racers did not do.

The End

Turn to page 70 to start the rough road race.

While you are waiting in line at the race committee table to go through the paperwork for the rough road race, you notice the sign over the officials' heads:

This race will test your skill, stamina, and nerves. Although it isn't anywhere near as fast as the speed race, it is still full of hazards.

Michael Reupleau motions you over to the table.

"It's time to choose now. What will it be? You can drive a British Land Rover or a Japanese Nissan Pickup. The other vehicles are already spoken for."

If you choose the Land Rover, turn to page 72.

If you choose the Nissan, turn to page 76.

You choose the easier valley route, which is surer, but longer. You will have to push yourself and keep moving at all costs to minimize the disadvantages of the longer course.

Finally you come to a major river crossing. The water is shallow and looks easy to cross. It appears that you're the only drivers to have come this way. There are no tracks on the riverbank.

You plunge ahead with the Nissan in low-range, four-wheel drive. The river bottom is pretty stable and solid. The water appears clean and clear. The river deepens towards the middle, rises to cover the hubs, and then recedes as you climb the opposite bank.

On the other side, Amos says, "I think it would be wise to stop and grease the hubs and axles, and the ball joints. Sand and silt can destroy these sensitive points."

You ask yourself, "Does the Nissan really need it? Is it worth the time?"

If you take the time to grease, turn to page 88.

If you decide the water was clean and you need to keep moving, turn to page 90.

You choose the British Land Rover. As you walk over to the garage to check its preparation and meet your co-driver, you glance at your wrist chronograph. Only three hours till you're scheduled to start. The paperwork with the officials took longer than you expected. You're hoping to get a navigator you can work well with. There are a lot of details to iron out before the start, and not much time to do so. All you know about your navigator is the name on the stick you selected. Eduardo.

At the garage—a long steel Quonset hut—a mechanic in greasy coveralls points out your car. Your Rover, a red one with a white top, is jacked up in the air. One mechanic is busy with a grease gun under the car; another, waving a large wrench around, is having an involved conversation with someone wearing a driver's suit. His back is to you.

That must be your co-driver. It sure looks like the Eduardo you know, but can it be? He would have let you know he was going to be here.

The mechanic with the wrench smiles and waves. The driver talking to him turns around. It is Eduardo!

You and Eduardo have driven together before and work well as a team. In addition, Eduardo has had lots of experience on rough roads, driving Jeep tours in the Colorado Rockies.

You and Eduardo hug each other heartily.

Turn to page 74.

"What are you doing here?" you ask him. "Why didn't you let me know?"

"I just got here this morning," Eduardo answers. "I didn't know I'd be here myself." His voice becomes quieter. "I'm substituting for somebody who was killed in one of the races." Then his face brightens. "Enough of that. We'll save the rest of the explanations for later. We have lots of work to do."

"How's the car?" you ask Eduardo.

"In good shape. Hank and Bill are almost done. All the mechanical systems check out. Hank is finishing the chassis grease job, and Bill and I are having a little argument about what weight motor oil to use."

You listen to the argument for a few minutes, decide Bill is right, and tell him to get on with it. Then you and Eduardo sit down with the maps and discuss routes, speed strategies, and what supplies and spare equipment to take.

Go on to the next page.

Before you know it, the starter has dropped the flag, and you and Eduardo are off. You have decided to take a paved road out of Nairobi for eight miles or so and then head off into the wilds. But you don't get more than four miles out of the city before you spot trouble ahead. A wooden barricade lies across the road, and soldiers in khaki are standing stiffly at attention.

You stop near the barricade and consult with the colonel there. He tells you in a stiff British accent that the route you want to take is blocked by thousands of drought refugees from the south. He says you might be able to continue the way you've planned, but that an alternate route he traces on the map may be better.

If you decide to continue on your original route, turn to page 78.

If you decide the colonel's route is better, turn to page 81.

You choose the Nissan. It's a beauty—red paint with gray trim. Race-prepared, it has heavy grills over the headlights, extra wheels, jerry cans of gas, a pickaxe, shovels, and a regular axe strapped in the bed. The whole vehicle smells of polish and motor oil.

While you are looking over the Nissan, a tall African man seemingly appears out of nowhere.

"Hello. You are holding a stick with my name on it, yes?"

"I have a stick with the name Amos on it. Are you Amos?"

"Amos Tutuola Msindai. I was named for the Nigerian novelist." He sticks out his hand. "Very glad to meet you. Shall we continue with our inspection?"

Finally your start time arrives, and you're off!

The Nissan runs wonderfully. Once you're free of the hubbub of the start, your first choice becomes clear. The route through the hill country is well-defined, but extremely rough. It is much shorter than the route through the valley. Normally you'd pick the easier valley route, except that it's poorly marked and has many river crossings that could be difficult.

If you choose the rough ride through the hill country, turn to page 86.

If you choose the longer valley route, turn to page 71.

"OK, I'll do it. I can use the money."

"Good for you, friend. I knew you'd see the wisdom in my suggestion," Ian says, chuckling.

"Now, Uzzi here, he'll fix you up. Right, Uzzi?"

Uzzi grunts and opens up a canvas drawstring bag. You see the sparkle of sunlight on diamonds. Uzzi trickles several diamonds into your outstretched hand, the little stones are sharp against your skin.

You decide not to tell Amos. At the end of the mandatory hour rest stop, you and Amos drive off slowly.

Turn to page 100.

It would be a waste, you decide, to throw out all the advance planning you and Eduardo did and stray from your original route.

You put the Rover into first gear, wave goodbye to the colonel, who stiffly salutes back, and drive around the barricade.

Several miles down the road you encounter the refugees. There aren't many at first, but the farther you drive the more you see. They're very thin—except for most of the children who have swollen bellies, a symptom of starvation.

The walkers look straight ahead as they trudge along, showing no curiosity about you, as though they had no energy to spare.

Before you know it, you're surrounded by refugees. You're forced to shift down into first gear. Then even that is not slow enough, and you must shift into your low range. Still the refugees come, and eventually you are forced to stop.

Turn to page 80.

You wonder if you should have taken the colonel's advice. You're having a hard time concentrating on the race with all these empty, gaunt faces surrounding you. The vultures circle overhead.

You're almost overwhelmed by the feeling that you must help these people, but what can you do? Your food and water supplies are limited; offering any to them would be a cruel joke.

If you decide you must stop and try to help the refugees, turn to page 84.

If you decide to go on with the race, but promise yourself that you'll return and help as much as you can, turn to page 91.

The colonel's argument for taking another route is persuasive. After some consultation with him over your map, you turn the Rover around and head back a short way down the road, looking for the dirt track the colonel described to you. In the rearview mirror you can see the colonel waving good-bye.

"Not more than a half mile back," the colonel had said. "Turn left at the baobab tree. The track is not well-marked, but you should be able to find it."

The tree appears right on schedule. The road seems to be nothing more than two barely worn tracks in the grass, but the colonel called it quite passable, and said it led directly to the river crossing you were heading for.

The road is even better than the colonel promised. Before you know it, you are at the river crossing.

"I wish the colonel had gone over our whole route with us," Eduardo says, turning around to look back at the road you've just driven. "That road was great!"

"Maybe that was great, but this isn't."

Eduardo whips around to see what you're talking about.

Turn to page 83.

In the middle of the river you see the ferry taking a passenger car across to the other side. It will be close to a half-hour before you can get a ride across. What makes it worse, though, is that the passenger on the ferry—which holds only one car—is a BMW SUV, the car driven by the team from Libya. The BMW SUV started before you did and you are not racing head to head, but it is still infuriating to see your competition in front of you.

Eduardo correctly points out that, if you've come upon the BMW SUV, you're ahead in the race and can afford to wait for the ferry. On the other hand, if you head down the river bank, then strike off for the next crossing, you may gain even more time.

If you decide to head toward the next crossing, turn to page 95.

If you decide to wait for the ferry, turn to page 98.

You are overwhelmed by the feeling that you must stop and help now. You tell Eduardo you have decided to abandon the race. You can't go on in the face of all this misery.

You step out of the car, full of regret at leaving both Eduardo and the race.

"I wish you luck, friend. Please do not feel bad about leaving me. I understand," Eduardo says.

You scarcely have time to wave good-bye before the press of the refugees pushes you on. You feel better with each step you take back toward the barricade. When you get there, you will volunteer to help with every ounce of your strength.

The End

Head for the hills! Take the chance—sometimes that's what makes the difference whether you win or lose.

The Nissan is easy to handle, and you and Amos are pleased at your overall progress. The sun is hot, but you two have been so involved in the race that you hardly notice it.

"My friend, there is a time checkpoint ahead. The rules call for a mandatory one-hour stop. We can use it."

A few minutes later, you come to a group of huts used by the Masai each spring. Several Jeeps and Rovers are parked under shade trees. You check in and chat with the race officials. They're non-committal about your overall progress in the race.

"Well, I guess they have to be that way. Right, Amos?"

He nods agreement and heads off to get water. You walk over to a green-and-blue Land Rover parked in the sun away from the other vehicles. Two men are sitting in it listening to a news broadcast.

"Welcome, friend. Come aboard. How about a beer?"

The smiling speaker is large, ruddy-faced, and in his fifties; he smells of beer. His companion is a wiry, dark-skinned man, who does not smile. You refuse the beer, but accept their offer to listen to the news.

Go on to the next page.

Several minutes pass. The ruddy-faced man, whose name is Ian, begins to speak in a low tone, apparently to no one in particular.

"They say somebody whose kneecaps are broken never walks—or drives—again." Ian turns to you.

"Got a deal you can't refuse, friend. Easy. No trouble. Nice money. Right up your alley."

You listen, wondering what's coming next.

"It's like this. My friend Uzzi here, and I, we have a bit of an investment in this race. Our car is a sure winner. I mean a sure winner. Get my drift?"

You feel very uneasy. You don't like this burly man named Ian or his silent friend.

"Right up front, friend, that's old Ian for you. We would like to 'donate' five thousand pounds— that's about ten thousand dollars in U. S. money— as a consolation to guys for not winning this race. Simple, easy, no problems. Deal?"

What now? You are being offered a bribe to throw the race. The race officials weren't encouraging about your progress in the race; you might just lose anyway. And if you turn Ian down, it sounds like he'll stop you some other way.

What should you do?

If you accept the bribe, turn to page 77.

If you refuse the bribe, turn to page 101.

88

You decide you'd better grease the car's fittings now. You can't afford to risk a breakdown later on.

Actually, it doesn't take long at all. And it's a good thing you chose to do it, too. When you inspect the grease oozing from the hubs, you find more contamination than you expected.

Then you are off in good spirits. Even the sun is cooperating. It seems less hot than before.

Toward 2:00 PM you arrive at a small ravine. You stop at the edge to select the best way across. The rainstorms have cut so severely into the reddish earth that part of one bank has broken away.

Then you see it! A skull! A human skull lies partially uncovered, staring with empty eyes at the ever-changing cloud patterns in the blue African sky.

"Amos! Amos, look!"

"Oh, my. What is that?"

You scramble out of the Nissan and kneel next to the skull. You dig carefully around with your pocketknife and discover several more skeleton fragments just beneath the earth.

"Amos, this could be the find of the century!"

"What do you mean? Aren't these just old bones?"

"Amos, this skull could be millions of years old. It could be the missing link between apes and people, one of the first real human species." The two of you examine the skull, noting its particularly heavy brow and shallow eye sockets.

Go on to the next page.

"No question about it, Amos. This is for real. We could be famous."

"Yes, yes, my friend, but we must hurry now. We are losing valuable time here."

Should you go on now and come back later with archaeologists? Or would it be better to give up the race? Your find might be much more important.

If you continue the race and plan to return later, turn to page 112.

If you abandon the race to further investigate your discovery, turn to page 105.

"To heck with the grease," you tell Amos. "We can make it."

You push off from the riverbank, making good time through the dry brown-yellow grassland. Gradually the grassland becomes desert. Your wheels kick up a lot of sand that gets into the suspension. It doesn't take long before you hear a horrible noise, like fingernails on a blackboard. It's the tearing sound of the sand coming into direct contact with metal.

Can you make it to the next checkpoint before making repairs? If you think so, turn to page 115.

Should you make repairs now? If you think that is best, turn to page 102.

You decide that there is not much you can do for the refugees now. There are so many of them and only one of you, but you tell yourself you will come back when the race is over and help somehow.

The crowd of refugees is so thick you can't move the car forward. Each minute that you must sit and watch these poor people makes you wonder if you're making the right decision.

Just as the horde of refugees thins out enough for you to get moving, you notice one poor family in particular: a man and a woman, each carrying a young child. As you get closer to them, the man gently puts down the little girl he is holding and then suddenly throws himself in front of your car.

You have just enough time to swerve out of the way, but not enough time to plan where to go. You run over a large rock. There's a loud crack and the Rover comes to a quick stop.

You and Eduardo hop out of the car. The man who threw himself at the car is lying face down in the dust, but you didn't hit him. Your tire track is several inches from his outstretched body. His wife hasn't even stopped; she is still walking down the road carrying one child and holding the other's hand.

The man gets up, and without looking back at you, starts walking to join his wife. You start to follow, but Eduardo grabs your arm and stops you.

"Let him go. Let's look at the car."

Turn to page 93.

The Rover, it turns out, has a cracked axle. It's not badly broken, but it's useless as it is. While you and Eduardo are trying to decide what to do, a military caravan drives by. One of the trucks stops and a young lieutenant jumps out. You explain what happened and what your problem is. The lieutenant listens quietly, then starts giving orders. Soon, before your astonished eyes, four soldiers are busy crawling under the Rover with a portable welding rig and some steel stock.

The lieutenant explains with a grin, "I've always wanted to be in this race. Helping you makes me feel as if I am in it."

Turn to page 94.

Turning serious, he also explains that the man who threw himself in front of the Rover was trying to get killed, believing that if he succeeded you would take pity on his wife and family and give them some money.

Just then, one of the soldiers who had been working on the car marches over, salutes, and, announces that the repairs to the Rover are finished.

The three of you walk over to inspect the axle. The chief mechanic proudly shows off his handiwork. He reminds you, though, that while his repairs are strong, the axle will never work as well as it did before.

"In other words," the lieutenant says, "watch out for large rocks."

You and Eduardo climb back into the Rover and wave goodbye. The lieutenant and his crew shout "Good luck!" and "Godspeed!" as you take off down the road.

Remembering the warnings of the lieutenant and his mechanic, you don't want to drive too hard. On the other hand, Eduardo is also a fine mechanic, and he thinks the repair to the axle is plenty strong and will hold through anything.

If you decide you'd do better to take it easy for a bit, turn to page 103.

If you agree with Eduardo and decide to push the car as hard as you can, turn to page 107.

Sitting around waiting for the ferry is no fun, you decide. You tell Eduardo you've made up your mind to keep moving.

You take off down the riverbank, following the river for about a mile and a half to where it makes a great bend. There you head off across the country to meet the river where it loops back.

There is no road where you want to drive, but the map shows your chosen route to be mostly grassland, so the going shouldn't be too rough. By keeping an eye on the dashboard compass, you keep going in the right direction.

You ford a number of little streams on the way, but they are no problem. The hardest part is choosing the quickest way through the trees.

Finally you cross one more stream, and you're on an immense plain. The map shows this to be the last veldt before the river crossing. At Eduardo's suggestion, you've put off greasing the car after each stream crossing until now, the last crossing for awhile. So while Eduardo is crawling under the car with the grease gun, you climb onto the roof to look around. Off in the distance to the north, you can see a herd of giraffes grazing the trees. Ungainly as they might seem, you are startled by their grace as they move about in search of food.

Once Eduardo is done, you take off immediately. You're impatient to continue.

Turn to page 96.

Soon you enter some high grass, which reaches almost as high as the hood of the Rover. The farther you go, the higher the grass gets, until you can barely see and have to slow down.

Suddenly you spot a rhinoceros in the brush not more than 100 yards away. It doesn't see you yet. You know a rhino will chase a car even without being provoked, and that it can catch up to one, too. Three tons of automobile is not a match for four tons of angry rhino.

If you stop the car, maybe it won't see you and will keep moving off in the direction it is going.

If you decide to keep driving and figure the rhino won't charge, turn to page 106.

If you decide to give the rhino the right of way and allow him to pass before you continue driving, turn to page 116.

You decide to wait for the ferry. As you watch it progress across the river, you see that it is going faster than you thought it could. Maybe you won't lose all the time you made up, after all.

While you and Eduardo are waiting, you decide to grab a bite to eat. There is a food vendor near the ferry landing and from him you buy several plantains—a type of banana—that he fries for you in palm oil heated in a metal drum over a wood fire. You also buy some hot tea with honey, and with some crackers and cheese from your supplies, you make a fine meal.

By the time you are finished eating, the ferry has returned and you drive aboard.

The ferryman chocks the wheels of the Land Rover and starts his little outboard motor. The ferry heads out through the shallows to the deeper water near the other side. Just as you get into deeper water, about a third of the way across, there is a muffled explosion. The ferry immediately lists to starboard.

The ferryman starts screaming and swearing. You and Eduardo run to the starboard side and lean over. Eduardo sniffs the air carefully.

"Plastique. Our competitors appear to be playing dirty."

Go on to the next page.

"Will we stay afloat to the other side?" you ask.

"Doesn't look like it. The explosive blew out most of the flotation. We'd be lucky to make it back to the shore we left, let alone the rest of the way across."

"Let's go back. Even if we don't make it all the way back, we'll be all right. The water is shallow there, and if we can't drive the Rover out, we can winch it out."

You explain to the ferryman with gestures and by pointing that you want him to return to the shore you left. He refuses and seems even more scared at the thought of going back than sinking in the middle. You're sure he won't go back because he is afraid he'll lose his fare. You promise him you'll pay him anyway, but it is no use; he won't turn around.

You don't want to lose the car. You must act quickly!

If you decide to overpower the ferryman and head back to the shallows, turn to page 108.

If you decide the ferryman is right in continuing into deeper water, turn to page 118.

100

Now it's up to you to lose the race! You dawdle on the road, trying to keep Amos from getting suspicious.

"What is this, my friend? Have you lost your nerve? You go as fast as a snake in cold weather. We need speed now."

"Can't. Car is acting up. Have to take it easy," you mutter.

Later that day, having lost hours on the wrong routes, you approach a steep gully. You can only cross it at one point.

You stop the Nissan and jump lightly to the coarse, dry grass on the edge of the gully. When you look up you see Ian and Uzzi. Why have they followed you? Ian is not smiling now.

"Diamonds, please," Uzzi orders, hand outstretched.

You run for it, but the roar of a Magnum is the last thing you hear. Ian slips the diamonds out of your pocket.

Amos escapes into the thick scrub underbrush. Ian and Uzzi search but never find him. Maybe he will avenge your death. But what good will that do you?

The End

"Sorry. Can't help you out," you say.

Ian's smile freezes and then disappears. He begins speaking in a voice that is almost mechanical.

"Listen and listen well. You do what we want or . . ."

Just at that moment a race official approaches you. He has a serious look on his face.

Should you tell the official about the bribe attempt? Will you get into trouble? Will your position in the race be jeopardized?

If you decide to tell the official, turn to page 111.

If you remain quiet, turn to page 120.

It takes three hours to pull the axles and hubs for the repairs. But you persist, and finally the job is finished.

You push on.

After fourteen-and-a-half hours of the hardest driving you've ever done, you cross the finish line. You are exhausted, hot, hungry, and happy.

Even though you have not finished first, or second, or even third, you have done well in one of the world's most grueling races.

The End

Turn to page 6 to start the speed race.

Even though Eduardo is sure that the soldiers' repair is more than strong enough, you feel that it will be safest not to pull out all the stops.

Each time you stop at a checkpoint, you examine the repair for signs of weakening. The welded axle holds perfectly, though, even when you bottom out in a particularly bad gully in the Olduvai Gorge. Eduardo spends an hour dragging, jacking, and pushing while you stand on top of the car and watch for puff adder snakes and other dangers.

Dusty, tired, and happy, you finally cross the finish line two days after you start. You finish fourth overall. "Not as good as first place," you think, "but at least we made it. That's better than many of the others."

The End

Turn to page 6 to start the speed race.

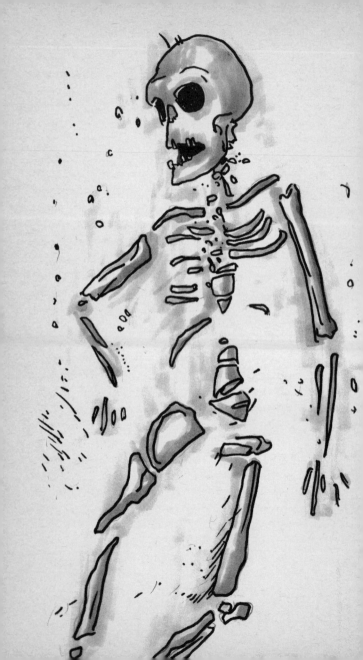

"Amos, I'm giving up the race. This is too important. We're standing in the Olduvai Gorge, where Louis and Mary Leakey discovered the bones of the earliest humans. This is where human life on earth may have begun."

Amos nods with understanding, and returns to the Nissan to radio in your withdrawal from the race. You tell him to report mechanical troubles as your reason. No sense in attracting too much attention to your discovery, at least not yet.

You study the skull and what appears to be an entire skeleton, as you sit for hours on the side of the gully holding the remains of your ancestor. You notice from the skull that its brain must have been small. What did this person see, feel, and do?

Near dusk you return to the Nissan. Just as you are about to enter the truck, you are struck by the vicious fangs of the puff adder—one of the world's deadliest snakes. As you drift into unconsciousness, you think about the first humans. Are you so very different from them? Then you see a brilliant white light. Your life ends here where humanity began.

Years later a student of the Leakeys rediscovers the site—and the remains are among the oldest human bones this world has ever seen. He knows about your death here because he is an amateur car racer himself, and he names the site after you.

The End

106

"I can outdrive any rhino ever born," you promise Eduardo as you shift into first and step on the gas.

The rhino looks up at the loud noise of the engine. Then, bellowing with rage, he charges at the car.

"Faster!" Eduardo cries. "It's gaining on us."

You speed up, and the rhino drops back a little.

Then, without warning, a hole appears right in front of you. There is no time to swerve. You drive right into it.

The front wheels of the Rover bottom out, and you pitch over. It's too bad that you never refastened your seat belts after the grease job. You are both flung from the car.

The rhino flattens you into such a pulp that not even the vultures are interested in you. The ants, however, have a field day.

The End

"The repair will either hold or it won't," you tell Eduardo. "If it breaks, we've had it. If it holds and we go slow, we've had it. Let's go all out."

For the next two days you travel as fast as you can over all kinds of terrain, driving up steep mountains, through baking hot valleys strewn with boulders, and across lush grasslands. You spot—and sometimes narrowly miss hitting—all kinds of wildlife: giraffes, antelopes, hyenas, even lions.

At last you roll across the finish line and accept the congratulations you deserve. You have finished third in one of the toughest races ever held.

The End

Turn to page 6 to start the speed race.

"There's no way we'll make it to the other side," you tell Eduardo. "We'll lose the car, not to mention maybe our lives. We've got to take control."

Again you try to convince the ferryman to turn around, but he looks even more scared this time. You signal Eduardo, who sneaks up on the man from behind and knocks him out with a monkey wrench.

Quickly you turn the ferry around and head back. At first it looks as if you'll make it, but then, with a sigh of escaping air, the ferry settles into the water.

Although the current is fast, the water is only about four feet deep. You're quite sure you can

winch the Rover out of the river. First, though, you have to get the unconscious ferryman ashore.

As you and Eduardo are carrying him, you hear splashes near the riverbank. Crocodiles! That's what the ferryman was afraid of, not losing his fare! You and Eduardo scramble to get ashore, but it's too late.

The last thing you ever see is a crocodile's tail flying toward you. After you're safely stashed underwater by the crocodiles, they'll spend the next few weeks devouring you slowly, piece by piece.

The End

You look at Ian and Uzzi and then at the race official, a man with a military bearing who exudes confidence. You speak up loud and clear.

"These men are trying to bribe me."

Of course Ian and Uzzi immediately deny it, but the race official calls over three constables dressed as local herdsmen.

"Good for you. We've wanted to catch these two for some time."

You promise to testify at their trial. Then it's time for you to take off again. Amos seems to have a sixth sense for navigating. The two of you don't miss a trick.

Eleven hours later you cross the finish line in Nairobi. You are the winners!

The End

Turn to page 6 to start the speed race.

112

You decide to go on with the race. You can come back with an archaeologist later.

The Nissan stops at the edge of a dry river. "Time to refuel," Amos announces. While you pour gas in the tank, Amos stretches his legs by walking in the riverbed. Suddenly he starts running toward you.

"Look, look! Gold! Gold! My friend, there is gold here!"

You run to meet him. Amos holds up a nugget of gold that must weigh four ounces.

You both start digging. More nuggets! There is gold everywhere.

"We will be rich. Let's quit the race now."

"But, Amos, we've come so far already . . ." you say doubtfully.

Amos doesn't answer but keeps digging up gold nuggets.

If you decide to go for the race rather than the riches, turn to page 121.

If you quit the race and hunt for more gold, turn to page 122.

You decide to push on, but it's a bad decision. There's too much sand in the suspension. You finally come to a grinding halt. You try to radio for help, but atmospheric conditions interrupt your broadcast. You'll have to wait it out.

At first you sit outside, but you're forced to move into the vehicle when a sandstorm roars up out of the south. You fall asleep during the night, and you, Amos, and the Nissan are buried in a sand dune for all time.

The End

116

By the time you get the Rover stopped, you're 150 feet from the rhino.

The animal is slowly moving away from you, swinging its massive head with the huge horns. It looks very much like a four-legged tank. It's the biggest rhino you've ever seen or heard of.

"That front horn must be four feet long," you whisper to Eduardo.

"And the body must be fifteen feet or more," Eduardo whispers back.

Suddenly, the rhino turns and looks toward the car. You can hear it snort: "Chough, chough, chough." Its beady little eyes seem to glare at you. Then, without warning, it starts charging.

Before you can even think of starting the car and driving away—if you could even get away—the rhino is upon you. They can move fast! The rhino comes so close you can feel its hot breath through your open window. At the last possible moment, though, it swerves and lumbers away from you.

"Phew! That was close," Eduardo says. You just nod agreement. Fear has frozen your vocal cords.

After a few minutes you feel better, and you start the car. Before you drive off, you buckle your seat belts. You discover that when you left the last stream crossing in a hurry, you had completely forgotten to fasten them. It was a good thing the rhino swerved. There's no telling what might have happened if you had both been thrown from the Rover.

Go on to the next page.

Once aboard the ferry at the river crossing, you and Eduardo check your maps carefully. You discover that you're making great time.

When the ferry reaches the other side, you're off even before it's tied to the dock.

Soon the terrain changes drastically, and you are picking your way over a rock-strewn trail in the Olduvai Gorge. Africa, you discover, is not only the steaming jungle you had envisioned. Your course takes you over lush plains teeming with wildlife, hot deserts that seem to hold nothing but sand, rugged, rocky hills and deep gorges strewn with boulders bigger than the Rover, and poisonous scorpions and puff adder snakes sunning themselves. There are lakes, swamps, and, yes, jungle. Africa has everything, you decide, much more than you imagined.

Throughout your journey the Rover performs wonderfully, running perfectly through the dark cold of the night and the daytime heat of the desert.

You continue to push yourself, Eduardo, and the Rover to the limit. At each checkpoint you find that you are doing well. Even though it comes as no surprise at the finish when you are declared the winner, it still feels very, very good.

The End

Turn to page 6 to start the speed race.

118

"The ferryman knows what he's doing," you tell Eduardo. "From the looks of him, he's been at it for a hundred years."

But when you get further into the deep water and sink lower and lower, it looks as if you were wrong.

A freak change in the current pitches the ferry over. The Rover and the three of you are dumped overboard.

The Rover sinks immediately. You and Eduardo start swimming for shore, dragging the ferryman with you, for it appears he cannot swim.

The current is swift, and the swimming hard. You are swept a long way downriver before you can climb ashore.

The ferryman is so grateful to you for saving him that he would do anything for you.

After you are rested, you start walking back to the ferry landing, where you hope to catch a ride to Nairobi. The rough road race is over for you, but at least you and Eduardo are safe. You'll be able to race again.

The End

Turn to page 6 to start the speed race.

The official looks the three of you over carefully and then speaks in a British accent, "Everything all right here?"

He pauses, waiting for your response. For a moment you almost decide to report them, but a quick look at Ian's menacing face makes you change your mind.

"Everything's fine. Just talking about the weather broadcast," you say.

The race official does not believe you. These men are notorious gamblers. They've been followed for several years by Interpol, the international police network. The official radios to headquarters that you are to be barred from the race.

There is nothing you can do. Your race is over.

The End

"I insist, Amos. I left the skull behind, remember? Let's go on with the race. We will come back for the gold later."

You do return after you have finished the race. This time you're equipped as a gold miner and prepared for a month of digging. You spend the month, but not as you had planned because you never find the gold again. It's as though it has vanished.

Too bad—but at least you placed in the top ten in one of the world's most challenging endurance races.

The End

"Forget the race," you say. "Gold is gold, right?"

You and Amos stake a claim, start mining for gold, and become extremely wealthy. Amos buys a villa in Monaco. You take up residence in the Bahamas. You two start your own series of races called Gold Fever.

The End

CREDITS

This book is the work of many people. R. A. Montgomery reviewed and edited the original manuscript, bringing it into the Internet age. Shannon Gilligan was executive producer. Laura Arnesen, Melissa Bounty, James Woodard and Susanne Pingree at Chooseco LLC and Judy Cooper, Kate McQuade, Marlene Stemple, and Ellen Maxwell at Sundance Publishing nursed it through various stages of editorial and artistic development. Stacey Hood at Big Eyedea Visual Design in Bigfork, Montana, was responsible for layout and design. Sally Reisner proofread and corrected the final words. Caitlin LaBarge provided invaluable final input as our 'cold reader'. Laura Sanderson kept everyone informed and on track. Gordon Troy performed the legal pirouettes that result in proper trademark and copyright protections. Last but not least, Sherry Litwack and Bob Laronga at Sundance acted as godparents. *A very special thanks to Wick Van Heuven.*

Illustrator: Sittisan Sundaravej (Quan). Sittisan is a resident of Bangkok, Thailand and an old fan of *Choose Your Own Adventure*. He attended The University of the Arts in Philadelphia, where he received his BSC in architecture and a BFA for animation. He has been a 2D and 3D animation director for productions in Asia and the United States and is a freelance illustrator.

Illustrator: Kriangsak Thongmoon (Tao). Kriangsak is a graphic artist living in Thailand. After attending Srinakarinwiroj Prasarnmitr University in Bangkok, Kriangsak made a career illustrating for various well-known publications in Thailand before switching his concentrations to 3D modeling and computer animation. However, his love for drawing and sketching still keeps him coming back to non-computer generated illustrations.

ABOUT THE AUTHOR

R. A. MONTGOMERY has hiked in the Himalayas, climbed mountains in Europe, scuba-dived in Central America, and worked in Africa. He lives in France in the winter, travels frequently to Asia, and calls Vermont home. Montgomery graduated from Williams College and attended graduate school at Yale University and NYU. His interests include macro-economics, geo-politics, mythology, history, mystery novels, and music. He has two grown sons, a daughter-in-law, and two granddaughters. His wife, Shannon Gilligan, is an author and noted interactive game designer. Montgomery feels that the new generation of people under 15 is the most important asset in our world.

**For games, activities and other fun stuff,
or to write to R. A. Montgomery,
visit us online at CYOA.com**

Look for other titles available now!

CHOOSE YOUR OWN ADVENTURE® 8

THE CLASSIC SERIES IS BACK!
CHOOSE FROM 27 POSSIBLE ENDINGS.

ESCAPE

BY R. A. MONTGOMERY

Look for other titles coming soon!

Look for other titles coming soon!

Look for other titles coming soon!

CHOOSE YOUR OWN ADVENTURE® 11

THE CLASSIC SERIES IS BACK!
CHOOSE FROM 22 POSSIBLE ENDINGS.

TROUBLE ON PLANET EARTH

BY R. A. MONTGOMERY

Look for other titles coming soon!

Look for other titles coming soon!

CHOOSE YOUR OWN ADVENTURE® 13

THE CLASSIC SERIES IS BACK!
CHOOSE FROM 23 POSSIBLE ENDINGS.

THE MYSTERY OF URA SENKE

BY SHANNON GILLIGAN

CHOOSE YOUR OWN ADVENTURE® 14

THE CLASSIC SERIES IS BACK!
CHOOSE FROM 19 POSSIBLE ENDINGS.

THE CASE OF THE SILK KING

BY SHANNON GILLIGAN

Look for other titles coming soon!

Look for other titles coming soon!

Look for other titles coming soon!

THE BRILLIANT
DR. WOGAN

BY R. A. MONTGOMERY